Niizh

Nadine Labelle

Dedication

Almost everything I write is dedicated to our two beautiful children. May you grow up strong and proud.
I love you!

XOXOX
Mom

Glossary of Ojibwe Words

Ambe - Come
Aanii – Hello
Enh – Yes
Ka - No
Miigwetch – Thank you
Ndaanis – My daughter
Niizh – Two
Semaa – Tobacco

Table of Contents

Nadine Labelle

Raven in the Window

I looked out the window of our minivan. Beyond my reflection and the rain trailing down the pane of glass, two eyes watched me. I blew a puff of hot air on the window and it fogged over. I took my finger and traced the silhouette of the bird.

"That crow is watching me," I said.

"What? Who is watching you?"

"That crow."

My dad turned his head and looked out the window.

"It's not a crow, it's a raven."

He turned back to the handheld computer in his hands.

"That raven is watching me."

Dad ignored me. I wiped the moisture off the window with the sleeve of my coat.

"Are you watching me, Raven?" I asked.

The black bird opened its big black beak and I could hear the loud caw softly through the window.

I lifted my hand and waved at the bird. The bird tilted its head to one side, extended a broad black wing out to the side and shook it.

"Hey, Dad! It waved at me."

"Um, hum," muttered my Dad. I heard the familiar jangle of his usual game. I wouldn't get much out of him for the next twenty minutes or so.

"Can I get out and stretch my legs?"

"Sure, Ndaanis. Just don't go far."

"I won't," I promised.

I pulled on the handle and stepped down, right into a puddle.

"Awww, nuts!"

I shook my dripping foot once I reached the other side. We were parked at the far edge of the grocery store parking lot. My baby brother was napping in his car seat while Mom had gone in. We were waiting out here like we often did.

I crossed the wet grass and squatted down to look at the raven. It hadn't flown away. In fact, it seemed to be waiting for me.

'Aanii, Raven, my name is Jade."

"Aanii, Jade."

I gasped in surprise.

"You talk!"

"Enh," agreed the bird. "Do you want to fly with me?"

"Really?"

"Enh."

I nodded my head and replied, "Enh! Yes!"

"Ambe," waved the raven launching into the air.

I followed Raven into the field, following as fast as my feet would allow. I let my fingers drag along the tops of the grass and in the next moment, as I looked down, I was above the ground. I was flying!

"Ambe, Jade!" coaxed Raven.

I flapped my arms and looking out side-to-side I saw that my arms were sleek black wings. I was a raven too.

I felt the power of the wind with each lift of my wings. With each push, I climbed up and up.

Feathers had looked delicate and fragile when I'd found them on the ground, but here, as I whistled through the air they felt strong and solid. They curved to cup the wind and lifted me higher and higher with barely an effort.

Alone, one feather was as flimsy as a blade of grass. A single feather would have bent and split. The wing, with all the feathers aligned was light and strong. My muscles controlled the movement of all the feathers and they worked together with grace and power.

Raven climbed and climbed while I followed.

We flew right through the clouds into the brilliant sunlight above. It warmed my feathers even as I was chilled by the crisp and cold air around us.

"Watch this," said the raven and suddenly stopped flapping. I mirrored Raven's movement and with wings slightly bent, we fell. It was stomach lurching and the most fantastic feeling of freedom, like a rollercoaster without the lap bar.

At last, as we broke through the clouds. Raven and I tilted our wings to catch the wind. We spiraled down and down in big lazy circles. When we nearly reached the ground we tilted our wings forward and skimmed the wet tops of the grass. The rain glistened and fell off our feathers like tiny jewels.

"This is amazing, Raven!"

"Now you know how to dance," replied Raven.

We reached the top of the world again and started the freefall. We tilted and weaved around each other. We spiraled together like we were dancing on the air. As the ground came closer, I realized we were back where we'd started.

Mom was lifting bags out of the cart and starting to arrange them in the back of the minivan. My dad was calling my name and had started to walk into the field.

I tried to call out to her, "Mom! Hey, it's me!"

What she heard was, "Caw! Caw, caw, caw!"

Raven laughed at me, "She can't hear you."

With tilted wings, Raven caught up to me. Raven did a summersault around me and vaulted back into the air towards the field.

"Ambe, Jade."

I followed Raven back towards the field. We flew over my dad's head and landed out of sight, further down the field. As my claws touched the ground they transformed back into feet with one wet and one dry shoe. As my wings lowered I wriggled fingers that felt very strange and tingly.

"Miigwetch, Raven!"

Raven cawed back at me and launched back into the air. I turned and started running back towards the van.

"There you are, Jade! We've been worried. We're ready to go," said Dad.

"Coming!"

Dad held out his hand and I reached out to grasp it. We walked hand-in-hand back to the van. Mom was just closing the rear hatch and moved the cart out of the way.

"I'll put it back, Mom," I said rushing forward to take the cart. I hurried it across to the shelter.

"Miigwetch!" she said closing the sliding side door behind me.

I slid back into my seat next to my baby brother. He had hardly moved the entire time. I buckled my belt and looked back out over the field. Mom pulled her sunglasses off the visor and pushed them onto her nose while Dad resumed playing his game. The sun was starting to come out.

"The strangest thing happened while you were out looking for Jade," she said.

Dad looked up for a moment with a curious expression, "Oh?"

"Yeah, two ravens flew out of the clouds and spiraled down above the van. It looked like they were dancing. It was beautiful!"

"Jade mentioned she saw a raven earlier. They must live around here."

"I think one lives around here, I saw it in the field," I supplied.

I looked out the window as we started moving and I saw a shadow spiraling down through the clouds. The wings tilted back and forth, like when an airplane says hello or goodbye.

"Mom, I want to dance this summer." I said, suddenly.

"You do?" she asked, surprised. She had wanted me to dance for several summers and I'd always refused.

"We can ask Auntie to make you a Regalia."

"Yeah, I want to be a fancy shawl dancer."

Mom glanced back at me and smiled as we pulled out of the parking lot.

The black shadow spiraling up through the clouds got smaller and smaller as we drove off. I started to imagine my shawl with a raven design. I imagined the brilliant blue of the sky above the clouds. It would be the background. The shining orange and yellow sunlight would be shown by the ribbons sewn along the edge of my shawl. The black raven's wings would reach from fingertip to fingertip.

"I know exactly what I want, I want wings!" I said.

"You'll be a beautiful dancer," Mom replied.

I watched Raven in the window as we drove away.

Voices on the Water

"I'm old enough to take the canoe out myself."

"No, Drake, I don't like the idea."

"But I want to go fishing."

"Can't you find a friend to go with you? Maybe Uncle Dave will take you on the weekend."

"What good is summer holidays if I still have to wait for the weekend to do anything fun! I'm going to go and hang out with Aaron instead.

"Everyone else is gone to do fun things, you know, like summer camp where they get to go canoeing and swimming all day."

"Oh, come on, Drake! You know we can't afford that this year."

I sighed, Mom didn't like Aaron very much either. He got kicked out of summer camp, she didn't want me to get into trouble.

"Yeah, I know Mom. It's not your fault, but I'm responsible enough. I promise to wear my life jacket at all times. I can't just sit at home all day, there's nothing to do here!"

Mom groaned and my heart leapt. She was weakening.

"If I'm old enough to stay home alone, aren't I old enough to go fishing? I'll bring home a big Pike for supper, you'll see."

Mom liked Pike, she licked her lips as she stuffed her work papers into her bag.

"You can make some scone to go with it."

She sighed. "Well, the weather is supposed to be nice and sunny most of the day."

"I'll just be gone a few hours and I'll call your cell phone as soon as I get back. I promise!"

"Okay, Drake."

"Yes!" I yelled, giving her a big hug. "Thanks, Mom!"

She laughed as I started to dance around the kitchen putting together a lunch. Nothing special, just peanut butter, and jam on whole wheat bread. I tossed it into a sandwich bag and I filled a water bottle from the tap.

"Have a good day, Honey," said my mom.

I rolled my eyes. I hated when she called me Honey. It wasn't like I was a little kid anymore. She kissed me on the cheek, grabbed her bag, her keys, and then she was gone.

I gulped down a glass of juice and a couple pieces of toast. I went out to the shed and it took all the power I had to drag out the dusty red canoe. I found two paddles, one for me and a spare. I tossed in my lunch and set my long green fishing rod on the far side.

I realized I would need bait, so I grabbed a little bucket, a gardening shovel and headed towards the flower beds. They weren't planted yet, Mom didn't have a lot of time to do those things. It was just the two of us.

Only a half dozen shovelfuls later, I'd found a dozen worms.

"Ready to launch!" I announced to no one in particular.

I packed the safety kit and buckled up the orange life jacket. I shooed a spider out over the edge of the canoe and pushed off into the water of Lake Huron.

I was still really shocked that Mom had let me go. I headed straight for my favourite fishing hole. It was across the bay where we live and at the edge of a shallow swampy area on what was basically just some rocks and shrubs.

It took about an hour to paddle out. There were always Pike in the reeds and I liked to just tie the canoe to an old gnarled tree and fish without worrying. I'd done it every summer with Uncle Dave for as long as I could remember.

I didn't notice the wind start to pick up. I had two Pike and a fat little Perch on the string, swimming alongside the boat. It wasn't until I heard a motor boat roar by my island that I looked out at all. The sky was a deep grey and the big water was choppy and white capped.

"Oh, no!"

I looked at my watch and realized it was almost two o'clock. Mom would be home by five and I'd better get moving. I was supposed to be home a couple hours ago earlier.

I pulled myself over to where my canoe was tied, I undid the knots and pushed off towards home.

I was only about five minutes into the paddle when the wind shifted viscously. I was pushed back to where I'd come from. The canoe rocked violently threatening to toss me overboard. I changed my strategy as the first crack of thunder rumbled over the water.

"Ambe! Over here!"

I heard a voice calling out to me. There was another small island nearby, mostly rocks, and I half paddled and was half pushed by the wind towards it. I was drenched in minutes and my muscles ached from trying to fight against the wind and water.

"Over here!"

"This way! You'll be safe here!"

I followed the faint voices towards the rocks. I was terrified that the canoe would be picked up by the waves and smashed. It would be hard to paddle and hard to get to shore if I had to swim. The rocks underwater would be covered in slime. Even with my life jacket, I knew I was in deep trouble.

"This way!" called the voices.

I didn't know what to do, I was panicking and the voices sounded so sure. Anything would be safer than not trying to do *something*.

I paddled towards where I thought they were, but I couldn't see anyone on the shore. All I saw were rocks. I fought with all my remaining strength to not get pulled past the island and pushed out into the open lake by the wind and waves.

As I got closer to the shore, I caught sight of a narrow channel. The rocks split in a skinny dark path that I hadn't seen from farther away.

As I fought against the wind I was finally able to fit my canoe into the crevice. I heard the voices again but I still didn't see where they came from. I was confused. There wasn't much of anywhere to hide in all the rocks and shrubs.

It was shallow and all the rocks worn smooth. The wind whipped at my hair and chilled me to the bone. My teeth were chattering to a point now that I couldn't think straight.

"Ambe!" came the call and like a zombie, I followed. I fought to get there.

At last it was shallow enough to climb out of the canoe and onto the rocks. There was a slight overhang that kept me a little dryer, but I was still standing in the lake as I looked around for the source of the voices.

In a flash of lightening, I pulled the canoe onto the rocks. I took some of my stuff, my paddles and huddled against the rock.

"You're cold," said a voice.

I looked around myself, expecting to see someone.

"W-where a-are y-you?"

"Here!"

"We are here."

I turned towards the voices, they came from behind me.

I turned and looked at the rock and in the glow of lightening saw the outline of two rock paintings. They were two creatures with long noses and teeth. I jumped as one of the heads turned to look at me.

"Aanii!" said the painting.

Something felt safe about these images on the stone. I'd seen similar ones in books and on TV. These ones were alive.

"Am I going crazy?"

"Ka."

The second image also turned. The eyes opened and closed and the mouths of the painting opened and closed like a cartoon.

"You are just lost."

"We have found you!"

"It has been a long time."

"Wholly, cow!" I said, my teeth chattering.

"It's not like it used to be."

"Ka, not like it used to be."

"What are you?"

"We are the ones who live here."

"Enh, we live in the rocks."

"We don't see the brave young boys anymore. We don't see the warriors or even the Shaman."

"Enh, it's very quiet now."

"It's too quiet now."

"We are very glad to see you."

"Enh, very glad to help you."

"Do you have any semaa?"

"Enh, do you have any semaa?"

"No, I don't have any of that."

"That's too bad," lamented one.

"That's very, very sad," lamented the other. "We like gifts."

"No one brings us gifts any more."

"Ka, no gifts. And we can't leave this place."

"We choose not to leave this place."

"Enh, this is our home."

"You're welcome to stay, until the storm is over."

"Enh, we will watch over you. You are one of our children."

I decided I liked the spirits. "I can share my lunch with you," I suggested extending a shaking hand with my slightly squashed sandwich.

"Lunch. What is lunch?"

"Food," I said.

"Food?"

"A sandwich. I mean, if you like peanut butter and jam."

The spirits were quiet for a moment and it looked as though they spoke to each other. The way the paintings overlapped was as though one listened to the other.

"We would like to try your lunch."

I pulled out the sandwich wrapped in plastic and tore it in half.

"Just a small piece."

"Enh, we only want to taste it."

"We know you will need the food too."

"Enh, eat your sandwich, but leave us just a small piece."

I tore off just a smaller quarter of the sandwich and left it at the base of the rock.

The thunder crashed and the lightening zinged with a crack into the lake. I shivered and pressed my back up against the rock, trying to huddle further under the over hang. I was still getting wet because the rain didn't just come down, it came at me from all directions.

The canoe rattled noisily against the rocks. There was a chance it could be washed away or damaged by huge logs and driftwood washed in by the waves.

"It's okay, you're safe here."

"Enh, you're safe with us, we've always watched over the people. Yes, our children. We think of you as one of them."

"You should rest. Come closer."

My eyes felt heavy. My arms and shoulders still ached and felt ten times as heavy as they actually were. I leaned against the rock and felt the warmth spread. The rock was warm where I rested. It was like it was alive and it was warming me. I shivered less and less, or at least I think I did. I fell asleep before I really knew what was happening. I was so tired. I slept and I didn't shiver any more. I was glad not to hear the thunder any longer.

"Wake up, Young Brave!"

"Enh, wake up, Young Brave."

"The storm is over."

"Enh, the storm is over."

It was the next morning and the sun was starting to rise and was turning the clouds pink and purple.

"It will be a beautiful day," whispered the voice.

"I survived?" I was lying in the dampness below the rocks and the paintings flickered like they were dancing just over my head on the stone.

"Of course you did."

I put my hand against the rock and said, "Miigwetch, Spirits in the rock."

"Go home, Young Brave."

"Come back again and bring us gifts."

"Enh, we like gifts."

"We like to be appreciated."

"It has been too long, we miss the People."

"I will come back again," I promised, "I'll bring you semaa."

"Good!"

"Very good!"

The fish I'd caught the day before still flopped around in the shallows where my canoe was banked. They too had survived the night and the storm. I pushed myself back through the narrow channel. I was so narrow I wouldn't have believed it was possible to travel through it during a storm.

I paddled and the sun started to dry my clothes. As I approached my house I saw the cars and search parties assembling to come out to find me. I waved to the people on the shore and watched as they scurried back to my house like ants, and some to the shore to meet me.

"I'm sorry Mom," I said giving her a big hug. Even though there were a lot of other people around, I didn't feel shy about crying as I hugged her.

"I brought you home the fish."

She laughed as she cried and hugged me.

All my family was there, passing along the news that I had been found on their phones and by yelling up to the new arrivals. It was nice to be appreciated.

"Where were you last night? I was so worried!"

"I'll tell you all about later," I promised, "And next time…"

"There won't be a next time," she said, "Drake, I was so scared!"

"Next time, I want you to come with me."

She smiled and laughed through her tears as we walked up the hill to the house with her arms wrapped around me.

"And Mom?"

"Yeah?"

"What is semaa?"

"Tobacco. Why?"

"Just wondering." I said. "I want to bring some with me the next time."

I was glad to get into our nice warm house and have a hot shower.

About the Author

Nadine Labelle is an Ojibwe from Serpent River First Nation living in Massey, Ontario. She is a free-lance writer and enjoys spending time in nature with her husband and their two young children.

www.ingramcontent.com/pod-product-compliance
Lightning Source LLC
Chambersburg PA
CBHW071231130626
46555CB00004B/1938